How Martha Saved Her Parents from Green Beans

BY David LaRochelle

PICTURES BY Mark Fearing

DIAL BOOKS FOR YOUNG READERS · an imprint of Penguin Group (USA) Inc.

To Debbie and Gary Barnes,
who make a mean green bean casserole
　　　　　　　—DL

For my big sister, Vickie,
and her garden of mean beans and crabby kale
　　　　　　　—MF

DIAL BOOKS FOR YOUNG READERS
A division of Penguin Young Readers Group • Published by the Penguin Group
Penguin Group (USA) Inc., 375 Hudson Street, New York, New York 10014, U.S.A.

Penguin Group (Canada), 90 Eglinton Avenue East, Suite 700, Toronto, Ontario, Canada M4P 2Y3 (a division of
Pearson Penguin Canada Inc.) • Penguin Books Ltd, 80 Strand, London WC2R 0RL, England • Penguin Ireland,
25 St Stephen's Green, Dublin 2, Ireland (a division of Penguin Books Ltd) • Penguin Group (Australia), 250
Camberwell Road, Camberwell, Victoria 3124, Australia (a division of Pearson Australia Group Pty Ltd) •
Penguin Books India Pvt Ltd, 11 Community Centre, Panchsheel Park, New Delhi - 110 017, India • Penguin
Group (NZ), 67 Apollo Drive, Rosedale, Auckland 0632, New Zealand (a division of Pearson New Zealand
Ltd) • Penguin Books (South Africa) (Pty) Ltd, 24 Sturdee Avenue, Rosebank, Johannesburg 2196,
South Africa • Penguin Books Ltd, Registered Offices: 80 Strand, London WC2R 0RL, England

Text copyright © 2013 by David LaRochelle
Illustrations copyright © 2013 by Mark Fearing

Designed by Jennifer Kelly

Manufactured in China

7 8 9 10

Library of Congress Cataloging-in-Publication Data
LaRochelle, David.
How Martha saved her parents from green beans / by David LaRochelle ;
illustrated by Mark Fearing.   p. cm.
Summary: A young girl must face her least favorite food
when a mean gang of green beans kidnaps her parents.
ISBN 978-0-8037-3766-2 (hardcover)
[1. Beans—Fiction. 2. Food habits—Fiction. 3. Parent and child—Fiction.]
I. Fearing, Mark, ill. II. Title.
PZ7.L3234Ho 2013   [E]—dc23
2012014361

The illustrations in this book were created
using traditional and digital tools.

Every Tuesday evening Martha's family had green beans for dinner.

Every Tuesday night
Martha was left alone
at the table, staring at
a plate of green beans
that she wouldn't eat.

"Green beans are good for you,"
said her mother.

"Green beans will make you big and strong," said her father.

They are both wrong, thought Martha. Green beans are bad. Very bad.

But even Martha did not know how bad green beans could be. Not until the day that a gang of mean green beans swaggered into town.

These beans had black beady eyes and long curly mustaches. They wore tall cowboy hats and sharp pointy boots.

They chased old ladies up
and down the street.

They threw rotten
tomatoes at the teachers.

4 + 4 =
3 + 3 =

They stormed into restaurants and tossed the cooks into garbage cans.

Anyone who had ever said, "Eat your green beans," was in big, **big** trouble.

Martha's parents were reading in the den
when the beans barged into the house.

The bad beans jumped on top of the furniture.
They tied her parents with long leafy vines.
They whooped and hollered and made rude noises.

Martha was in the kitchen staring at a plate of cold beans.

When she heard the ruckus, she ran into the den.

It was empty.

The front door was open and a note was tacked to the wall:

We have taken your parents. The Beans

No more parents meant no more nagging to clean up her room.

No more parents meant no more going to bed when she wasn't sleepy.

And no more parents meant no more green beans for dinner. Ever.

"Hooray!" shouted Martha.

She threw her plate of cold green beans right out the window.

Then she grabbed a box of cookies and settled on the couch to watch her favorite movies long past her bedtime.

Martha was
happy.

But not really.

She missed her parents
and wanted them back.
By morning, she knew
what she had to do.

She marched out of the house and followed a trail of leaves that led her to a cave. Outside the cave she saw her mother and father tied to a rock.

They were surrounded by hundreds of green beans, laughing, dancing, and singing off-key.

"Give me back my parents!" shouted Martha.
The beans did not even look at her.

"Untie them right now!"
The beans only snickered.

"Let my parents go,
or I will . . ."

"Or you will **what?**" said the beans.

"…or I will eat you!"
said Martha.

The air grew cold.
The singing and
dancing stopped.

The leader of the beans stepped forward and spat on the ground. "You will not eat us," he said with an evil sneer. "You have never eaten a green bean in your life."

He took a step
closer to Martha.

Then another.

And another.

With every
step the bean
seemed to
grow larger.

He climbed onto a rock and looked Martha in the eyes.
"You are too much of a **coward** to eat a green bean."

Martha's legs felt like melting butter. She wanted to run home and hide beneath her bed. But she pinched her nose, opened her mouth, and swallowed that bean in

one big gulp.

The other beans gasped.

Martha ate those
beans, too.

When she untied her parents, they hugged her and kissed her and told her that she was very brave.

crunch crunch crunch

From that day on, Martha's family never had green beans for dinner again. Instead they had broccoli or corn on the cob or a nice leafy salad.

Everyone knows that there is nothing bad about a nice leafy salad.